Fork in the Trail

by Laurie Calkhoven
illustrated by Arcana Studios

American Girl®

Published by American Girl Publishing, Inc.

Questions or comments? Call 1-800-845-0005, visit our Web site at americangirl.com, or write to Customer Service, American Girl, 8400 Fairway Place, Middleton, WI 53562-0497.

Printed in China
11 12 13 14 15 16 LEO 10 9 8 7 6 5 4 3 2 1

Illustrated by Thu Thai at Arcana Studios

Special thanks to Dr. Sandra Sawchuk, DVM

Welcome to Innerstar University! At this imaginary, one-of-a-kind school, you can live with your friends in a dorm called Brightstar House and find lots of fun ways to let your true talents shine. Your friends at Innerstar U will help you find your way through some challenging situations, too.

When you reach a page in this book that asks you to make a decision, choose carefully. The decisions you make will lead to more than 20 different endings! (*Hint:* Use a pencil to check off your choices. That way, you'll never read the same story twice.)

Want to try another ending? Read the book again—and then again. Find out what would have happened if you'd made *different* choices. Then head to www.innerstarU.com for even more book endings, games, and fun with friends.

Innerstar Guides

Every girl needs a few good friends to help her find her way. These are the friends who are always there for **you.**

A brave girl who loves swimming and boating

A confident girl with a funky sense of style

A good sport, on the field and off

A nature lover who leads hikes and campus cleanups

An animal lover and a loyal friend

A creative girl who loves dance, music, and art

A kind girl who is there for her friends—and loves making NEW friends!

A super-smart girl who is curious about EVERYTHING

Innerstar U Campus

1. Rising Star Stables
2. Star Student Center
3. Brightstar House
4. Starlight Library
5. Sparkle Studios
6. Blue Sky Nature Center

7. Real Spirit Center
8. Five-Points Plaza
9. Starfire Lake & Boathouse
10. U-Shine Hall
11. Good Sports Center
12. Shopping Square
13. The Market
14. Morningstar Meadow

You run across the Innerstar University campus, hoping to get to the Blue Sky Nature Center while your friend Paige is still working there. She's been showing you around the Nature Center, and it's quickly becoming one of your favorite places at Innerstar U.

Paige's enthusiasm for nature and the environment is contagious. You'll never look at a leaf, a tree, a flower, or even a bug the same way again after spending time with Paige. Blue Sky Nature Center is amazing, too. You especially love the courtyard filled with big trees and bright flowers.

As you step into the courtyard, you hear someone shout hello. You can't tell where the voice is coming from—behind the chestnut tree? Beneath the boxwood bush?

Then up pops Paige from behind a flower planter. She's covered with dirt and grinning from ear to ear.

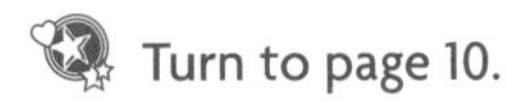
Turn to page 10.

"Hey!" Paige says, sliding off her gardening gloves and brushing her blonde hair out of her face. "Ready to check on the peppers?"

You nod eagerly and follow Paige into the greenhouse. It's filled with plants and vegetables, and you've become excited about watching them grow. You've even learned to like red and green peppers after helping to harvest them.

The sun and glass walls combine to make a great environment for growing plants, but it's a little hot for humans. Gazing through the glass, you notice how cool and inviting the woods behind the center look. You know there are hiking trails, but you haven't explored them yet.

Paige sees you staring at the trees. "Would you be up for an overnight adventure in the woods?" she asks.

Turn to page 12.

An overnight adventure!

Paige has been teaching you all about the trees and the wildflowers that grow in the woods, and you have been wanting to see them firsthand. You've also heard that the university has a campsite nestled deep in the woods. This could be your opportunity to check it out.

"I'm planning a hiking and camping trip for this weekend," Paige says. "I could really use a co-leader. How about it?"

"Really?" you ask. "Your co-leader?"

"My co-leader," Paige says again. Her brown eyes sparkle. "It'll be great. I'm sure lots of girls will want to join us."

Lots of girls? Your enthusiasm starts to fade. Leading girls on a hike in the woods is way different from studying plants in the greenhouse with Paige. Are you really ready to lead?

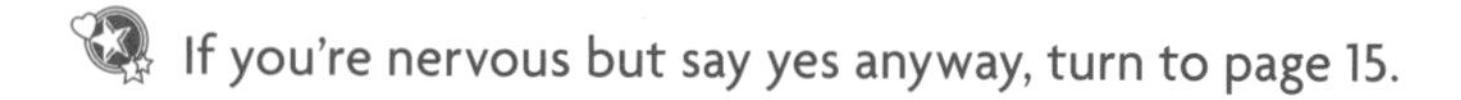

You have a great time playing soccer and even score a goal for your team. You notice that Riley goes out of her way to kick the ball to other girls so that they can make a play, even when she could easily make the goal herself. She wants everyone to have fun and feel included.

What a smart team leader, you think to yourself. *I'll have to try some of those things when I lead the hike.*

During a time-out, you tell Riley and the other girls about the hike in the woods and how fabulous it will be. Riley is as excited to go as you are.

After the game, you're hungry and ready for lunch at the Star Student Center. Then you remember your talk on hiking safety.

If you head to the library, turn to page 18.

If you decide to eat first, turn to page 28.

Paige is waiting for your answer.

"Are you kidding?" you say. "I can't wait."

You feel proud and flattered that Paige invited you to help lead a hike. You've never done anything like that before, but if Paige thinks you're ready, you must be.

"We should make some posters and see who wants to sign up," Paige says.

You're excited to help. "I'm on it!" you tell her.

You set out for one of the art rooms at Sparkle Studios. When you get there, you find Neely sitting on a bench with her sketch pad. Neely is one of the most creative people you know. If she's not painting or drawing, she's humming a tune or coming up with a dance routine.

"*You* look happy," Neely says with a smile.

"I am," you tell her. "Paige and I are going to lead a hike in the woods! I'm here to make posters for it."

"Want some help?" Neely asks.

"Sure!" you reply.

With Neely's help, you create posters to hang up around campus. And almost every girl you talk to says she'll come!

 Turn to page 16.

You head back toward your room at Brightstar House, uncertainty churning in your stomach. You told Paige that you'd lead this hike with her, but you're afraid you don't know enough to be a strong leader.

You barely notice the beautiful weather or the flowers and trees around you. All you can think about is how many things could go wrong. What if the other girls look to you for answers and you don't have them? You don't want to embarrass yourself. You also don't want to lead anyone into danger.

You decide to find your friend Shelby at Brightstar House and talk things over with her. Shelby always has great advice.

Along the way you pass Starlight Library. Maybe you should brush up on hiking safety instead?

If you look for Shelby, turn to page 17.

If you stop at the library, turn to page 20.

That night over dinner, you tell the girls at your table all about the hike. "It's going to be a great adventure," you say. "The Nature Center staff is going to set up the camp and have dinner waiting for us, so we won't have to carry too much. We'll explore the woods, see all the wildflowers in bloom, and sleep under the stars."

Your enthusiasm must be contagious. Even more girls sign up!

The next morning, you find Paige in the Nature Center and let her know how many girls are planning to join you. Many of them have never hiked or camped before.

"Wow, you did a great job," Paige says. "I wonder if we should put together some hiking safety rules so that the new hikers know how to stay safe."

Once again, you're excited to be able to help. "Great idea," you tell Paige. "I'll do it!"

You're on your way to Starlight Library to do some research when Riley runs up to you. She's out of breath.

"We need one more player for a soccer game," she says. "How about it?"

"I don't know," you say. "I've got some research to do."

"Just one game?" she asks.

Riley is so fun to play with that it's hard to say no.

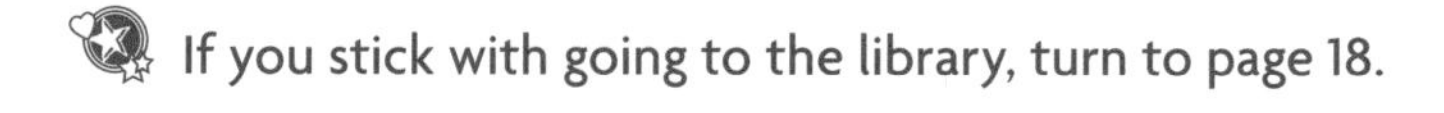
If you stick with going to the library, turn to page 18.

If you decide to play soccer, turn to page 13.

You find Shelby in her room. She listens carefully while you tell her how nervous you are about the hike.

Just talking about your worries makes you feel better. Then Shelby reminds you how much you've learned and how passionate you've become about nature. "That's what makes a good leader," she says.

"But what if the other girls expect me to know as much as Paige does?" you ask. "*She's* a great leader."

Shelby nods. "But there are different kinds of leaders," she says. "Paige is such a good hiker that I might not be able to keep up. I'd feel better if *you* were leading, too."

You never thought about it like that before. Paige might be the right leader for the experienced hikers, while you might be the best guide for the new hikers. Suddenly you can't wait for the hike!

Turn to page 23.

Starlight Library wraps around a courtyard filled with plants and trees. The courtyard is the perfect place to study on a nice day, but today you've got other things to do. You head inside to find a few books on hiking safety.

You curl up on one of the library's comfy window seats and start taking notes.

"Whatcha doing?" someone asks. It's your friend Logan. You should have known she'd be here. Logan is the most curious person you know. She's always checking out books or showing other girls how to use the library or the Internet to find answers of their own.

Logan is looking at the books on the seat next to you with an interested expression.

"Paige and I are going to lead a hike in the woods," you tell her. "I'm trying to put together a talk on hiking safety, but there's so much to learn! I don't know where to start."

"Start at the beginning," Logan suggests. "What's the most important thing for the group to know?"

You think about that for a minute and then realize you know the answer. "Stay together!" you say.

"Okay!" says Logan, grinning. "That's a good start. Now what else?"

With Logan's help, you put together a list of the top ten hiking rules, things like staying with the group and making sure to carry water and snacks. It's a great list, and you're excited about sharing it with the hikers tomorrow. You study the list for a while, trying to memorize it.

It's a funny thing, though: Focusing on hiking safety makes you start to think about everything that could go *wrong*. What if there's an emergency tomorrow and you don't know what to do?

If you push those thoughts away and tell yourself everything will be okay, turn to page 23.

If you find Paige to confess your worries, turn to page 22.

Top Ten Hiking Rules

1. Stay together (with the group).
2. Stay on the trail, and watch where you step.
3. Carry water and high-energy snacks.
4. Tell someone where you're going and when you'll be back.
5. Dress in bright clothes. Wear layers and sunscreen!
6. If you get lost, stay put and wait to be found.
7. Respect wildlife—don't touch or feed the animals.
8. Hike at a slower pace so that you don't run out of steam halfway through.
9. Bring out what you bring in—clean up.
10. Have fun!

You find a book on hiking safety in the library. You sit down in one of the comfy window seats to take some notes. You're starting to feel more comfortable—until you come to the section on first aid.

Fear starts gnawing at your stomach again while first-aid rules swirl through your mind. What if someone gets hurt and you can't remember what to do?

Your friend Logan comes by, sees your worried frown, and asks you what's wrong. Logan is curious about *everything*. She knows a ton of interesting facts, and she's a whiz at research.

But your questions today don't have anything to do with facts. You're worried about what kind of a leader you'll be. Can Logan help you with that?

If you share your concerns with Logan, turn to page 29.

If you find Paige and tell her you can't go on the hike after all, turn to page 22.

You and Paige have a short chat while the other girls gather around the puppy. Honey loves the attention. She's planting slobbery kisses on every hand that comes within reach of her mouth.

"What do you think?" Paige asks.

You're flattered that Paige takes the time to ask your opinion. "She sure is cute," you answer.

Just then Honey lets out a loud yip and strains against her leash. She wants to greet all the girls on campus.

You can't help but laugh. "I think she's a little over-excited," you say. "She could be a handful on the trail."

"You're right," Paige agrees. "Cute or not, we'll have to leave her behind."

Turn to page 40.

You find Paige in the Nature Center. You confess that you're afraid you don't have the leadership skills it takes to guide your classmates through the woods. You start listing all the things that could go wrong.

"Whoa!" Paige laughs. "Now you're scaring *me*!"

She sees how upset you are and gets more serious. "I was nervous the first few times I led hikes," she says reassuringly, "but the more time I spend in the woods, the more confident I become."

You're not sure you will *ever* be as brave and smart as Paige.

"If you still want to go on the hike, I can help you get ready," Paige offers. "Or we could take a short hike on our own before you make a final decision. How about it?"

If you take her up on her offer of a private hike, turn to page 32.

If you take her up on her offer to help you get ready in other ways, turn to page 33.

If you thank her but politely bow out of the hike altogether, turn to page 37.

The night before the hike, you knock on Paige's door to go over your safety tips and study the trail map.

"Hey, partner," Paige says with a smile. "Are you ready for our big adventure?"

"I can't wait!" you tell her. You step into Paige's room, which you love. She has pictures of trees, flowers, and animals on her walls and animal-print pillows on her chairs. There's a big "Save the Planet" banner hanging over her bed.

Paige spreads the trail map out on her desk and asks you what you think would be the best trail for the hike.

You're flattered. Paige has hiked most of the trails in the woods, but she still wants your opinion. Together you choose Blue Sky Trail, which looks the safest. Then you make a checklist of everything you need to bring along.

Back in your own room, you go to sleep confident that the hike is going to be super-fun—and safe!

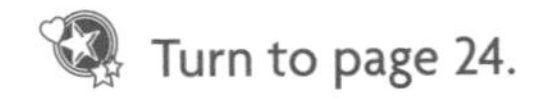
Turn to page 24.

Hidden Hills Trail
Starfire Stream
N
NE
E
SE
S
SW
W
NW

Turn to page 26.

The next thing you know, sunlight is streaming through your bedroom window. You get dressed, grab your backpack, and head for the Star Student Center.

You find the other hikers eating a hearty breakfast and packing lunches for the trail. Girls are chatting excitedly about the day ahead. Logan is on a mission to spot some birds along the trail and a constellation or two in the night sky. And Neely has a spooky ghost story ready to read by the campfire.

"Don't worry," Neely says. "It's not *too* scary." She makes a ghostly sound that cracks you up.

As soon as you and Paige finish your own breakfasts, Paige whistles for everyone's attention.

"My co-leader is going to clue you in on everything you need to know to stay safe on the trail," she announces.

You're a little nervous when you realize that all eyes are on you, but you pull out your list and start reading the top ten safety tips. You make up funny examples to illustrate your points, and pretty soon everyone is laughing.

Your friend Shelby asks you all to pose for a "before" picture for the yearbook, and then it's time to go. You slip on your backpack and join Paige at the front of the group.

Turn to page 35.

WELCOME
Campers and Hi
MILK
MILK

After lunch, you grab a few just-out-of-the-oven oatmeal cookies from the bakery and hang out with your friends on one of the terraces overlooking the campus. You're having such a great time that you decide to wait and head to the library after dinner.

Over dinner, Emmy talks about how much fun she's having pet-sitting Honey, a golden retriever pup. Emmy invites you to play Frisbee with them in the meadow tonight, and you instantly agree.

Honey is *so* cute, and she's a good Frisbee player, too. She races after the Frisbee and then brings it back to you in her mouth, her tail wagging and her eyes begging you to throw it again, *please*. You, Emmy, and Honey play for an hour, until Honey finally curls up in the grass and rests her chin on the Frisbee. She's exhausted.

You're tired, too. By the time you get back to Brightstar House, all you can think about is climbing the spiral staircase to your loft bed. Soon you're fast asleep.

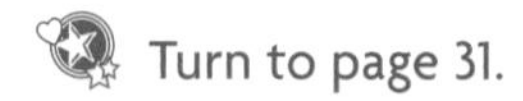
Turn to page 31.

Logan totally understands your fears, but she thinks you'll be a great leader for the hike.

"Paige wouldn't have asked you to help her if she didn't think you were ready," Logan says. "She's an expert on this stuff. But it might make you feel better if we print out some basic first-aid tips, so you'll have them just in case."

Logan helps you do an Internet search, and you make a checklist of everything you'll need for your first-aid kit. Even better, Logan tells you that she wants to come along on the camping trip. "I love sleeping under the stars," she says. "You can see the constellations so much better in the woods than on campus or in town."

"If you'll point out the constellations, I'll teach you all about the wildflowers along the trail," you say.

"It's a deal!" Logan says.

Turn to page 30.

You find Paige in the Nature Center putting up a display about trees and how good they are for the air we breathe. She created a poster of all the things girls can do to help the planet, topped by her personal motto: "Show the Earth some love. One girl *can* make a difference!"

Paige is impressed by your checklists. "I have a first-aid kit, but it's a great idea to have two in case we get separated. You've thought of everything," she tells you. "The only thing we have to do is go over the trail map and plan our route."

You agree to meet in her room at Brightstar House on Friday night, the night before the hike. In the meantime, you decide to study the trail map on your own so that you'll be ready with some ideas.

You're still a little nervous about being a leader, but you're definitely looking forward to Saturday. With an expert like Paige at your side and a little planning and preparation, you'll be brave enough to handle anything!

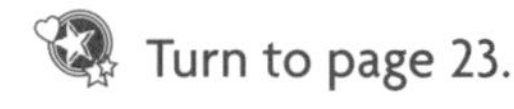
Turn to page 23.

Saturday morning dawns bright and clear. You can't wait to meet Paige and begin the hike.

You find Paige and the rest of your friends at the Star Student Center. They're eating breakfast and packing lunches for the trail. The Nature Center staff will bring dinner to the campsite, so you have to pack just enough food to get you there.

Paige whistles to get the hikers' attention. She tells them that you'll be clueing them in on everything they need to know to stay safe on the trail.

Uh-oh. You were having so much fun with your friends yesterday that you totally forgot to do your research!

Everyone is staring at you, waiting for you to speak. You can feel your face turning a deep shade of red. You're racking your brain for hiking safety rules, but you come up blank. All you can do is stammer.

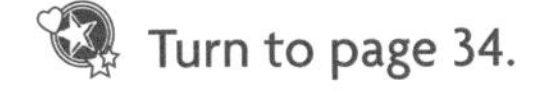
Turn to page 34.

On Friday, you and Paige finish your classes in the morning and then meet for lunch at the Star Student Center. Afterward, you pack some snacks for the trail, fill your water bottles, and set out on your private hike.

As you walk, Paige points out trail markers and gives you other tips for finding your way in the woods. You have a great time with Paige and learn a lot. When she almost steps into a patch of poison ivy, you spot it first and are able to stop her just in time!

As you head back to campus, Paige asks, "Do you feel ready now to help me lead tomorrow's hike?"

You barely need time to think about it. After today's hike, you've gained the confidence you were looking for.

"Yes," you tell Paige. "I can't wait!"

The End

Over the next few days, Paige helps you get ready for the hike. She gives you lessons in reading trail maps, spotting trail markers, and staying safe in the woods. She helps you put together a first-aid kit just like hers for your backpack.

Your friends are totally excited about the hike. Neely wants to sketch the wildflowers along the trail. Logan can't wait to sleep under the stars and look for constellations.

By Friday, you're beginning to feel ready, too. All the nervousness in your stomach has been replaced with excitement. You go to bed feeling confident that the hike is going to be a great adventure!

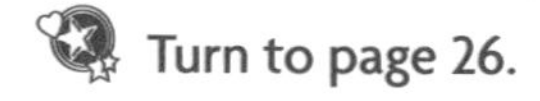
Turn to page 26.

Paige quickly realizes that you don't have a clue what to say. She speaks up and covers for you. "The most important thing is to stay with the group," she says.

You stand by red-faced while Paige gives the rest of the talk. You don't think she will trust you to help lead the hike after what just happened, and you're too embarrassed to tell her that you forgot to prepare.

You pull Paige aside while the girls finish making their lunches. "I'm sorry," you say. "I just didn't have time to put my safety talk together."

Paige says she understands, but she seems sad and disappointed. You're disappointed in yourself, too—so much so that you don't think you can go on the hike today. It would be too hard to spend the day with Paige, knowing how much you let her down.

You tell Paige that you're still really busy—you need to stay on campus today to finish some homework. As you watch her and the other girls leave for the hike, a sick feeling forms in the pit of your stomach.

The first step in being a leader is being prepared, you think. *And I definitely wasn't.*

You learned your lesson, but you let Paige down. You trudge sadly back to Brightstar House, hoping that you haven't lost a friend.

The End

You and Paige are leading the group toward the Nature Center when Emmy runs up with Honey, a golden retriever she's pet-sitting. The dog's tail is wagging nonstop.

"Can you take her on the hike?" Emmy asks. "I'd bring her myself, but I have a swim meet this afternoon."

Paige raises her eyebrows. "A puppy on the trail would be a lot of work," she says. Then she asks what *you* think.

You see Paige's point, but you don't want to disappoint the other girls, who really want Honey to come.

If you tell Paige you'll look out for Honey, turn to page 36.

If you talk it over with Paige first, turn to page 21.

Paige agrees to let Honey come, as long as you keep a tight grip on her leash. Honey stops to greet every girl you pass with a happy wag of her tail. She's slowing you down, but you think she'll be a lot of fun on the hike.

Your stomach flutters as you walk behind the Blue Sky Nature Center and step into the woods. It's a beautiful day, and you take a deep breath of the fresh air. The trees stretch to the sky, and birds fill the branches with their music.

Paige takes the lead, and you walk in the back of the group with Honey, making sure everyone stays together.

"What kind of trees are those?" Logan asks.

You're excited to realize that you know the answer. "That's a white oak," you say, pointing. "It can grow to seventy feet high. The one next to it is a walnut tree."

You've been on the trail for only a short time when a chipmunk darts across your path. With a bark, Honey races after the chipmunk. The leash jerks in your hand, catching you off guard. Before you know it, you're racing through the woods after Honey. She's straining at the leash. You're afraid that if you try to stop her too quickly, you might hurt her.

If you give the leash a hard tug, turn to page 38.

If you hang on for dear life, hoping Honey will slow down, turn to page 41.

Saturday morning, while all of your friends are happily heading to the Nature Center to meet Paige, you hide out in your room. You curl up with a book about rain forests and think about how lonely Brightstar House will be tonight.

I could have been out there in the forest instead of just reading about it, you think. You imagine all the fun everyone will be having without you. But then a list of all the things that could go wrong starts to run through your mind again.

At least you didn't lead anyone into disaster. *That* would have been really embarrassing. You tell yourself that you're glad you stayed behind. But deep down inside, you wonder if you really are.

The End

You pull back on Honey's leash, which slows her down for a moment. A rustling of leaves in the bushes ahead starts her off again. You race after her, dodging and ducking under limbs and branches.

"Honey, STOP!" you call to the pup, giving the leash another sharp tug. And it works! Honey stops in her tracks—just as you trip over a branch and fall flat on your face.

Honey runs back and starts licking your cheek, as if to say, "Let's race again!"

You can't help but laugh at her, but you also realize that bringing Honey along wasn't the smartest choice. You're going to have to take her back to campus.

You tighten your grip on her leash and then try to get to your feet.

Suddenly, getting Honey back to campus is the least of your problems. You've twisted your ankle! You need the help of a nearby tree trunk to stand. Will you even be able to walk back to campus?

"Uh-oh, girl," you say to Honey. "I need help."

Turn to page 47.

"Sorry," you tell Emmy. "I just don't think it's a smart idea. A playful puppy and a hike in the woods are a risky combination."

The hikers are a little disappointed, but they know you and Paige made the right decision. Emmy does, too.

You give Honey a scratch behind the ears and promise to walk her around campus another time. The puppy looks up at you and barks as if to say, *Okay!*

You and Paige lead the girls through the Nature Center greenhouse and out into the woods.

Turn to page 42.

You race through the woods after Honey. You snatch a quick peek over your shoulder and realize that you can't see the trail anymore. If you let go of the leash, you may never see Honey again. If you hold on, you may never find the trail again.

Suddenly, everything turns green. Honey led you right into a tree. At least it's an evergreen, a Douglas fir with springy branches. You don't get hurt—just a little scratched.

You're relieved when you look down and see that you're still holding the leash. Honey is waiting next to the tree with an expression that says, *Wasn't that fun?*

"No," you say. "That wasn't fun." But you can't help laughing at her silly face.

Turn to page 44.

Already the day feels magical as you walk under a canopy of trees. You name them as you walk: cottonwood, oak, and cedar. Birdsong mixes with the sound of leaves rustling in the wind, and you take a deep breath of fresh air.

Logan points to a bird on the limb of a cedar tree. "Is that a bluebird?" she asks. It drops to the forest floor with a musical *cheer cheer-lee chur.*

"That's definitely a bluebird," Paige tells her. "You can tell by its rusty orange chest. And there's a cardinal, too!"

Shelby snaps a photo before the bird flies away.

You close your eyes for a moment and listen to the secret language of the birds. Paige has been teaching you about them. After a few seconds, you're able to pick out a sound you recognize—a long trill. You look in the direction of the sound.

There it is in the branches above you—a thrush! You're about to point it out to Logan when—*splat!*—you trip over a rock and fall flat on your face.

If you rest for a moment to make sure you're not hurt, turn to page 45.

If you use a dead log to pull yourself up, turn to page 48.

You take a few minutes to catch your breath, tighten your grip on Honey's leash, and turn back in the direction of the trail. There's just one problem. You got so turned around in Honey's mad dash after the chipmunk that you don't know the way back. You don't even know which direction to go in.

Everywhere you look, you see trees and shrubs. Your heart starts to beat way too fast. It's your very first hike in the woods, and you've managed to get completely lost.

Calm down, you tell yourself. *Paige and the others will come looking for me.* But then you wonder if they'll even know where to *start* looking. You decide to make some noise.

"I'm here!" you yell.

Your shout makes Honey bark. She's so loud that you think your friends will hear her, but will you hear *them* if they're calling for you?

Honey finally quiets down, and you hear something. Is it a whistle? Is it a bird?

If you go toward the sound, turn to page 53.

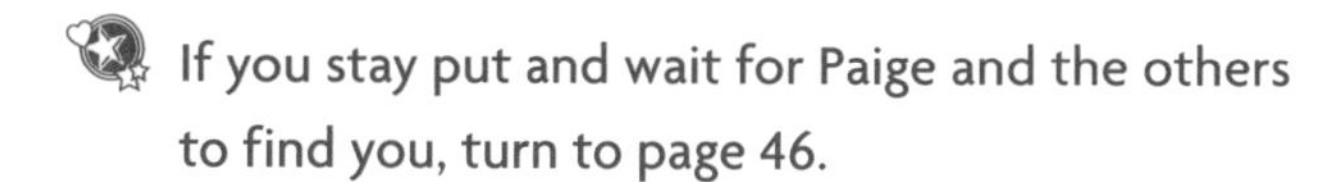

If you stay put and wait for Paige and the others to find you, turn to page 46.

You take a deep breath and focus on your body. You don't feel any pain. *That's a good sign*, you tell yourself. Then you notice the leaves you managed to plant your face in.

"Don't come any closer," you tell Logan. You recite the old rhyme with a groan: "Leaves of three, let it be—"

"Oh no!" Logan says.

Paige comes over to see what's wrong.

You sit up and point to the leaves, saying, "I forgot all about hiking rule number two: 'Watch where you step.' I've got poison ivy on my face and my hands. Itchy rash, here I come."

Paige is sympathetic. So is everyone else when they hear what happened. But you know you're going to have to return to campus. You take a moment to show the hikers what poison ivy looks like, and then you wave good-bye.

Going home early is a big disappointment, and before long, tears are slipping down your cheeks. It's hard to stay sad for long in the woods, though. Soon you spot a downy woodpecker, and a few minutes later, a deer mouse scampers across the trail.

When you notice another patch of poison ivy, you realize that you were a pretty good leader. At least you kept your friends from getting too close to the nasty plant. Next time, you hope you'll spot it before you land in it face-first.

The End

If you get lost, stay put and wait to be found, you remind yourself.

Honey sits at your side, tail wagging happily. You run your fingers through her fur. "I guess I can tell Emmy you got your exercise," you say with a laugh.

A few minutes later, you hear voices calling your name. The voices are coming from the same direction as the whistle you heard. Still, you're glad you didn't try to find the other girls by yourself. It's way too easy to get turned around in the woods.

You stand up and wave your arms, and soon you're reunited with Paige and the rest of the hikers on the trail.

Turn to page 56.

Honey seems to know that you're injured. She walks quietly by your side as you make your way slowly and carefully back toward the trail.

You think back to breakfast and your talk on hiking safety. What was rule number two again? Stay on the trail and watch where you step?

"At least I'll be able to show the girls what can happen when you *don't* follow the rules," you tell Honey.

You can see Paige walking toward you with Neely and Logan. All three of them start to run when they realize that you're hurt.

Paige kneels down to check your ankle. "Do you think it's broken?" she asks.

"No, I think it's just sprained," you tell her. "But it hurts too much to walk on it for very long."

Neely takes charge of Honey while Paige and Logan help you back to the trail.

Turn to page 49.

You place your hands on a dead log and push yourself up onto your knees. A wasp buzzes around your head, and then another. You hear a humming sound coming from inside the log.

Uh-oh. Your hands are just inches from a wasps' nest. And the wasps are getting very, very angry.

Slowly and carefully, you back away from the furious humming. Logan is stepping toward you to see what's going on, and Neely is right behind her.

"Stop!" you say, holding up your hand.

If you tell your friends to back away slowly, turn to page 50.

If you tell your friends to run, turn to page 52.

When you finally reach the trail, the rest of the girls crowd around you to see if you're okay.

"I'm fine, everybody," you say. "But I twisted my ankle. I'm going to have to go back to campus."

You give Honey a pat on the head. "Honey's coming with me," you say. "Curious puppies and hiking definitely don't mix. And on top of that, I broke my own rule—I didn't watch where I stepped! I tripped over a branch."

"I'll go with you," Neely says.

"Me, too," Logan adds. "You'll need help getting back."

You know that both your friends have been looking forward to the hike. Neely wants to sketch wildflowers, and Logan has been studying stars so that she could point out constellations tonight at the campsite.

 If you take them up on their offer, turn to page 54.

 If you try to get back to campus on your own, turn to page 55.

"Stay back," you say, nodding toward the log.

Logan grips Neely's arm to catch her balance. Neely's eyes get wide, staring at the wasps streaming out of the log. A few buzz around your head, warning you to stay away.

"Let's stay calm," you say. Then you remember your first-aid research. "Is anyone allergic?" you ask.

Logan shakes her head.

"I don't think so," Neely whispers.

"Move away slowly," you tell them. "Try not to make them any madder."

Finally, after an agonizingly slow walk away from the log, you're back on the trail and ready to catch up with Paige.

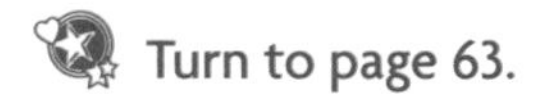
Turn to page 63.

The wasps are starting to pour out of the nest.

"Run!" you yell.

Logan and Neely do exactly that. You jump to your feet and run as fast as you can, too, but the wasps are faster. That's when you remember that running is the *wrong* thing to do when you're near a wasps' nest.

By the time you get back to the trail, you have a few stings. Luckily your friends got away sting-free.

Paige pulls out her first-aid kit to treat your red welts with soothing lotion. "Let's rest for a few minutes to make sure you don't have an allergic reaction," she says.

"I was about to plant my foot in the middle of that nest," Logan tells you while you wait.

Neely gives you a big hug. "You saved us with your quick thinking," she says.

Your friends' comments help take the "sting" out of your injuries. After a short rest, it's clear that you're not going to have a severe reaction. Your stings are red, swollen, and a little sore, but that's no reason to cancel your hike.

You jokingly begin a new top ten list as you continue on the trail to the campsite: "Top Ten Reasons for Watching Where You Step!"

The End

You move toward the sound, hoping it was Paige's whistle you heard and not a bird. You're feeling completely lost until you realize that you can follow your own path. You and Honey left a trail when you crashed through the brush. You can see broken twigs, crushed leaves, and even paw prints and footprints in the soft earth.

After a few steps, you hear girls calling your name. Honey starts running again, and you run with her. Before you know it, you're back on the trail, surrounded by your friends. Honey greets the girls with excited barks, but their eyes are on you.

"Are you all right?" Paige asks.

Logan gasps and touches your cheek. All of your friends are concerned about the scratches on your face and arms—courtesy of your run-in with the fir tree.

"I'm fine," you say with a laugh. "Girl plus dog plus tree equals lots of scratches, but it's nothing some first-aid cream won't take care of."

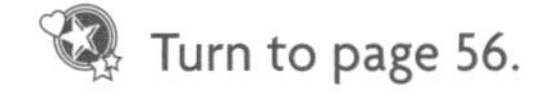
Turn to page 56.

You wish you didn't have to accept Neely and Logan's help, but you don't think you can make it back to campus without them.

Logan makes sure she has a firm grip on Honey's leash. "You're a troublemaker," she tells the puppy. Her tender tone of voice doesn't match her words. Neither does her friendly scratch behind Honey's ears.

Honey's response is a big slobbery kiss on Logan's hand.

You put one arm around Neely's shoulders to take the pressure off your ankle. Together the three of you say good-bye to the others and make your way back to campus.

You try to identify some of the wildflowers for Neely as you hobble along.

"That's a buttercup," you say, pointing to a yellow bloom. "And that one is called baby blue eyes."

"So pretty," Neely murmurs.

"I'll bring you back to sketch them as soon as my ankle heals," you promise.

After a short, painful hike, you're sitting safely in the nurse's office being treated for a sprained ankle. Logan and Neely leave to take care of Honey, but they promise to check on you later.

Turn to page 57.

You insist that you can make it back to campus on your own. You grip Honey's leash firmly as you wave good-bye to the girls. Honey looks up at you and whines.

"I made a bad choice in bringing you along," you say sadly. "I guess I still have some things to learn."

As you turn back on the trail, Paige suddenly runs up beside you. "We're coming, too," she says in a firm voice.

You feel a flood of relief, but also guilt. "I don't want to ruin everyone's fun," you say.

Paige throws her arm around your shoulders. "Don't you remember the first rule in hiking?" she says. "It's the *most* important thing."

Stay together, you think. You give Paige a grateful smile. She has taught you a lot about nature and leadership, but even more about being a good friend.

The End

As soon as Paige sees that you're not hurt, she asks what you want to do about Honey. She's much too nice to say, "I told you so," but you both know she was right all along.

"Curious puppies and hiking don't mix," you say. "I'm going to take her back to campus."

You know that if you take Honey back to campus, you'll have to sit out the rest of the hike. Walking back to campus alone will be all right—you haven't come very far. But you won't be able to turn around and catch up with the hikers. The group will be too far along the path, and you know that you shouldn't hike that far on your own.

You feel terrible about letting Paige down, but you have no other choice. You're about to say good-bye when Neely, Logan, and Shelby offer to go with you so that you can all hike back together.

If you insist that they go ahead without you, turn to page 58.

If you take them up on their offer, turn to page 59.

"It's only a minor sprain," the nurse tells you. "You did a great job of keeping weight off it after you fell."

"My friends helped," you tell her.

An hour later the nurse checks your ankle, and the swelling has already gone down. As long as you're careful, you can walk with crutches.

"Don't overdo it," the nurse warns.

As you make your way across campus, you realize that your leadership skills could use some work. You didn't listen to Paige when she said that bringing Honey along might not be the best idea.

You feel terrible about disappointing Paige. She counted on you to help her lead the hike, and now she's guiding the hikers on her own. You also ruined Logan and Neely's overnight adventure.

If you head to your dorm room to be alone, turn to page 60.

If you decide to find a way to make things up to your friends, turn to page 61.

You appreciate your friends' offer to go with you, but you don't want to ruin their hike. You wave good-bye and let them know that you can't wait to hear all about their adventure.

Your hike back is a short one, but it's long enough for you to think about your decision to bring Honey along.

"This isn't all your fault," you say to Honey. "Next time, I'll think things through and make better choices."

Honey wags her tail happily, as if she knows that she's forgiven. Then she spots another chipmunk.

"No way!" you say, gripping the leash and planting your feet. "This time, we're staying on the trail."

Honey whines, but she listens to you. You smile when you realize that you'll lead at least one hiker safely home—the one with four legs.

The End

Your friends assure you that they don't mind hiking back to campus with you and Honey.

"We haven't come very far," Shelby says.

"And my sketch pad is almost full," says Neely. "I need another one!"

"I wish I had remembered to bring a bird book with me," Logan adds. "Now's my chance to find one in the library."

Shelby slips her arm through yours. "See?" she says. "It's lucky for us that you have to take Honey back."

You're pretty sure your friends are just being nice, but you're grateful. You keep a firm grip on Honey's leash—you don't want any more off-trail adventures this morning—and you lead your friends back toward the Nature Center.

When you reach campus, you split up. Neely and Shelby run over to Sparkle Studios for art supplies, and Logan heads for the library. You walk Honey back to Emmy's room. The four of you agree to meet at the Nature Center in twenty minutes.

Turn to page 62.

You try not to make eye contact with anyone as you head to your room at Brightstar House. You're afraid that if someone asks you about your ankle, you'll burst into tears.

Quietly, you let yourself into your room and sink down into a chair. You wrap yourself up in a blanket and think about everything that went wrong today. You think about Logan and Neely, too, who are missing out on the fun because of you.

One tear slips down your cheek, and then another. You barely hear the gentle tapping on your door. By the time you limp across the room and open the door, there's no one there, but a gift from your friends is tied to your doorknob.

Something about those bobbing balloons lifts your spirits. Or maybe it's the thought of your friends—who are here for you through thick and thin. You wipe your face and remind yourself that things will look up tomorrow. You'll start again then.

The End

Now that your ankle is feeling better, you'd really like to find a way to have some fun with Neely and Logan. You have an idea, but you'll need some help.

You find your friend Isabel at Brightstar House and tell her what happened. "I feel terrible about Logan and Neely missing out on the hike," you say, "but I think I have a way to make it up to them." You tell Isabel your plan.

Isabel's blue eyes sparkle behind her glasses. "That sounds like fun," she says. "Count me in!"

You gather a few more friends. You talk to the staff at the Nature Center, too.

Before you know it, everyone has pitched in to create a little campsite right behind the Blue Sky Nature Center. You'll have the same fabulous dinner as the girls at the campsite, and the same dessert—s'mores!

As soon as everything is in place, you find Logan and Neely to announce your surprise.

Turn to page 64.

You beat your friends back to the Nature Center and take a minute to look over the trail map. The trail you and Paige chose is clearly marked and the easiest of the trails. There's a shorter path called Hidden Hills Trail that meets up with the other trail near the campsite. It looks more difficult, but it might allow you to make up for lost time. Should you take it?

You want to make the right choice. This is your chance to show your friends that you really *do* have what it takes to be a leader, even though you made a bad decision about Honey this morning.

Logan is the first to meet you at the Nature Center. Neely and Shelby are right behind her. You lead your friends into the woods for the second time today—this time without any four-legged friends.

If you stick with the original trail, turn to page 66.

If you take the shorter, steeper trail, turn to page 68.

Paige and the other hikers are in a small clearing surrounded by trees and wildflowers. It's a beautiful spot, but it has been ruined. It looks as if some people camped here and didn't clean up after themselves. There's trash littered all around the clearing.

Paige doesn't get angry about too many things, but when people treat the environment badly, she gets steamed. Now she's fuming.

You pull a few trash bags from your backpack and hand them around. "No worries," you tell Paige. "We'll clean it up!"

"Good thinking," Paige says.

You're proud that you remembered to bring trash bags along. Soon everyone is pitching in to pick up the garbage.

As you toss a can into your bag, you spot a plastic bag way off the trail rolling in the breeze. It disappears behind a bush. You're tempted to go after the bag, but there's plenty of trash to pick up right here, and you don't want to get separated from the group.

If you chase the bag, turn to page 74.

If you let it go, turn to page 69.

You knock on Neely's door. When she opens it, you're happy to see that Logan is there, too.

"Hey!" says Neely. "We were just on our way over to see how you're doing."

"The nurse said it was only a sprain," you say. "I'm really sorry that you missed the hike because of me."

"It's okay," Neely says, giving you a hug.

"There will be lots of hikes," Logan says. "But you only have two ankles!"

You giggle. Then you tell your friends that you have a big surprise for them.

"What is it?" Neely asks.

Logan and Neely are full of questions, but you won't say a word—not until you've led them slowly down the path to the campsite behind the Nature Center.

"Ready to camp out?" you ask them with a smile.

Logan and Neely run to join the other girls. They're *so* happy and excited, and that makes you feel good.

That night you lie in your sleeping bag, listening to Logan name the constellations. This isn't the campout you expected, but it's still pretty cool.

Wow, you think. *I made all this happen. Maybe I'm not such a bad leader after all.*

The End

You set out on Blue Sky Trail again. As you hike, you and Logan look for more birds. Soon you've spotted robins, a blue jay, and a chickadee.

Neely is itching to sketch the wildflowers. Shelby, who is almost never without a camera, snaps lots of pictures. Soon she and Neely are planning a joint collage of sketches and photos.

You're glad you decided to stick with the original trail. You spot Paige long before her group of hikers would have reached the point where the two trails meet.

You're about to shout hello when you get a look at Paige's face. Even from a distance, you can tell that something is wrong.

Turn to page 63.

You want to impress Paige, so you make up your mind to hike Hidden Hills Trail. You lead the girls up a small rise. Already it's clear that this trail is harder than the other one. It's much hillier.

Logan notices, too. "Isn't this a different trail?" she asks.

You show the girls your trail map and explain your plan to surprise Paige by catching up with her super fast.

Neely points to the spot on the map where the two trails meet. "What if they're waiting for us below this point?" she asks. "They're probably going kind of slow so that we can catch up."

Neely, Logan, and Shelby look to you to make the decision.

Wow, you think. *They really do trust me to be their leader, even though I made the wrong choice about Honey.* That makes you doubly determined to make the right choice this time.

 If you go back to the original trail, turn to page 70.

 If you stick with the new trail, turn to page 71.

Pretty soon, with teamwork, you've picked up all the trash. You and Paige check the trail map and see that you've come almost halfway! Everyone is hungry after all that work. And now that the clearing is cleaned up, it's the perfect place to eat your picnic lunch.

As you sit and eat your sandwiches, the birds chirp overhead. The magpies seem to be waiting for you to drop some crumbs.

A butterfly flits past. "Look, a painted lady," Paige says, pointing to an orange and black butterfly.

Shelby snaps a few photographs. Neely sketches a picture of a butterfly perched on a wildflower. Then she uses a colored pencil to get some rubbings of different leaves, too.

You sit back and take it all in. You're surprised to discover that watching your friends have fun is a lot of fun for *you*, too. *Maybe that's what being a good leader is all about*, you think to yourself.

You check the trail map again. Neely is totally right.

"That's true," you say. "If Paige and the others decide to wait for us along this part of the trail, we could miss them completely. Good thinking."

"I'm only following your own safety tips," Neely says with a laugh. "Remember what you said this morning? 'Make sure someone knows where you're going.'"

"That's right!" you say. "I almost broke my own rule. Let's go back to Blue Sky Trail."

Shelby links her arm through yours as you hike back in that direction. "We can still surprise Paige with how quickly we catch up," she says sweetly.

Turn to page 66.

You're really looking forward to showing Paige that you can be a good leader. You think that making up time by taking the harder trail will prove that. You decide to stick with the new trail.

"Paige won't slow down the whole group to wait for us," you tell Neely. "She's not expecting to see us again until we reach the campsite. Just think how surprised she'll be when we get there so quickly!"

The new trail is hillier and narrower than the original. One hill is so steep that you have to stop to rest halfway up. You finally reach the top, only to discover a fork in the trail that's not on the map.

You're nervous about leading the girls in the wrong direction, but you also don't want them to know that you might be lost.

If you take the path to the right, turn to page 76.

If you take the path to the left, turn to page 80.

After lunch, all the hikers make sure they've packed up their garbage to carry out with them. You don't want to leave anything behind for animals to get into! Then you and Paige lead the way.

You've walked for about an hour when you come to a fork in the trail that's not on the map.

"One of these must be an old path," Paige says. "But which one? They both look a little overgrown."

"There's one way to find out," you say. "What if we each take a buddy and walk for fifteen minutes? We can meet back here and then figure out which way to go."

Paige is reluctant to split up the group, but she agrees that it may be your best option.

Riley volunteers to be your buddy. Shelby is going to hike with Paige, and the rest of the group will wait for you at the fork.

"Left or right?" Paige asks you.

If you take the path to the left, turn to page 82.

If you take the path to the right, turn to page 84.

INNERSTAR UNIVERSITY

You run off the trail, following the plastic bag. You're about to pick it up when you see it scurry away from your hand. It's as if the bag has legs. Wait—it does! That's when you notice the black and white fur. A *skunk* is stuck in the plastic bag, trying to get free.

Paige is always telling you how trash is bad for animals. Here's the perfect example. The poor skunk is stumbling around, rubbing up against rocks and a tree trunk to try to get the bag off.

You're scared. You know it's a bad idea to approach a wild animal, but it's hard to run away from the skunk when you know that it's in trouble.

The skunk shakes its head wildly, and the bag catches on a fallen branch and finally slides off. The skunk looks a little dazed but happy to be free.

The bag is within your reach. You're tempted to grab it so that other animals won't get caught in it, but you don't want to startle the skunk.

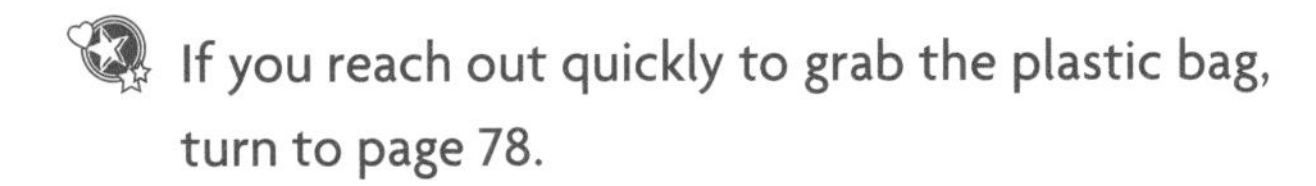
If you reach out quickly to grab the plastic bag, turn to page 78.

If you run before the animal notices you, turn to page 81.

You lead the girls along the path to the right. The trail gets narrower, and you start to wonder if it's really a trail at all. You're scared now, but you don't want the other girls to see that. You bury your face in the trail map.

Logan studies you. "Is something wrong?" she asks.

You can't look at her. "We're lost," you finally confess.

At first, the other girls seem as anxious as you feel. Then they start throwing out ideas. This time, you listen. Shelby suggests that you climb a tree to see where you are.

You carefully climb a sturdy pine, but you still can't see anything. Beneath the sound of rustling leaves, you think you hear a stream. There *is* a stream on your map, and the original trail runs along it for a stretch. If you can find the stream, you might find the trail.

You're climbing down, ready to share your good news, when Neely says, "Hey, look! Bigfoot was here."

Bigfoot? You shimmy down the tree and study the footprint. Suddenly you realize what it is. An icy chill passes through you. "Umm, that's a black bear paw print," you say. "We'd better get out of here—fast!"

If you head for the stream, turn to page 83.

If you head back in the direction you came, turn to page 85.

You reach out to grab the plastic bag. It's stuck on a twig, which breaks with a sharp *snap!* The skunk hears the sound and whirls around.

Uh-oh! You take a step backward, but you trip over a branch. Before you can get to your feet, the skunk defends itself the only way it knows how. It lifts its tail and sprays.

The smell hits you before you can say a word or call for help. By the time Paige and the others come running, the skunk is gone. But the smell lingers.

Paige stops short with a horrified expression. Riley clamps her hand over her nose. It's clear that you can't keep hiking. You need a shower—and fast.

Shelby and Riley offer to walk back to campus with you while the other hikers eat their lunch.

You're sorry to be missing out on the campout, but you've definitely had enough adventure for one day. You've learned a couple of things, too. Now you know *why* you should always stick to the trail and keep your distance from forest friends. By the "smell" of things, you don't think you'll be forgetting those rules anytime soon!

The End

You head left and hike a long way along the trail. Finally, you come to a Hidden Hills Trail marker. You're on the right path. Phew! But the hike is steep and hard—much harder than the original trail. You won't catch up to Paige anytime soon.

You come to what seems like the top of the hill. It's hard to tell with all the trees blocking your view. Everyone is huffing and puffing, so you decide to stop for a rest.

"Let's have our picnic," you suggest.

You settle under the trees and unpack your sandwiches. Neely eats quickly so that she'll have time to sketch some wildflowers. She searches the brush on the edge of the trail.

"Hey!" Neely calls out suddenly. "Come look at this!"

Turn to page 101.

You take a step backward, but your movement scares the skunk. It starts running away—toward the other girls. You have to warn them!

"Skunk!" you yell. "Skunk!"

There are so many screams and squeals that the skunk takes off in the other direction.

"Phew! That was a close call," you say.

Everyone gathers around to hear about your encounter with the skunk. You can tell that Paige is impressed by your quick thinking.

"That's why you should never get close to any wild animals," you say. "Epecially the smelly ones!"

The girls giggle with relief and then get back to business. There's still garbage to be picked up.

Turn to page 69.

You and Riley head off to the left.

"Maybe we should mark our path as we go," Riley suggests, "just in case this isn't the main trail."

You hesitate. "The path seems pretty clear to me," you say, "and we're not going too far."

"I guess you're right," Riley agrees.

Riley is a strong athlete, and you're glad to have her with you when the trail suddenly gets steep and narrow. You're about to suggest turning back when you hear the snapping of twigs. Something is running toward you.

"What's that?" Riley asks, her eyes wide.

A deer bounds up, stopping a few feet away from Riley. You don't know who's more startled—you, Riley, or the deer. The deer turns and runs the other way. You and Riley glance at each other and grin.

"This can't be the main trail," you say, catching your breath. "I think more deer use this path than people! Let's go back to the fork and tell the others."

Turn to page 87.

You hike toward the sound of the stream as fast as you can. Every crackle in the underbrush makes the four of you jump. You keep scanning the ground for more bear prints, hoping not to see any. Luckily, you don't.

Finally, you reach the stream, but there's no sign of the trail. Should you head left and walk upstream, or head right and walk downstream following the flow of the water?

You decide to ask your friends. All four of you study the trail map, but none of you has a clue where you are.

"I don't know," Neely says, rubbing her sore feet. "You guys decide."

Logan thinks heading upstream will bring you closer to the campsite. Shelby thinks that if you hike downstream, you'll find the spot where the two trails meet. The decision is yours.

If you go downstream, turn to page 88.

If you go upstream, turn to page 92.

If you sit tight and wait to be found, go online to innerstarU.com/secret and enter this code: BSMARTBU

You and Riley start hiking the trail to the right. It's clearly marked, and you have no trouble following it. "This is definitely the main trail," you tell Riley. "Paige and Shelby must be hiking an old path. Let's go back."

You hike back to the fork and wait there with the other girls. Ten minutes pass, and Paige and Shelby haven't returned. You wait another fifteen minutes, and they're *still* not back.

Now you have to figure out what to do. With Paige gone, the other girls are looking to you to lead them.

You and Riley decide to hike the trail to the left to look for Paige and Shelby. You move quickly, until the path becomes steep and narrow. As you stop to catch your breath, you think you hear the sound of voices.

"This way," you say to Riley. You're in a hurry to find your friends, but luckily you take the time to check your footing. You see that some dense bushes are hiding the edge of a ravine.

Paige and Shelby weren't so lucky. They're at the bottom of the ravine, and it looks as if Paige is hurt. She's sitting on a rock, holding her wrist.

Turn to page 90.

You and the other girls jump at every noise, convinced that you're going to come face-to-face with a hungry bear. You're still making your way back to the fork in the trail when you hear something running toward you.

Neely shrieks and grabs your arm. "Is that a bear?" she whispers.

You can't answer. You don't know.

Logan throws her arms around Shelby. But Shelby, always the photographer, raises her camera. She's ready to take a picture.

Suddenly you see a deer bounding through the woods. Is it running away from something? You hold your breath, expecting to see a bear chasing after the deer. But there's nothing. After a few seconds, you can breathe again.

You start hiking again on shaky legs. Finally, you come to a fork in the trail. Is it the same one you followed earlier? It's hard to tell. Should you go uphill or downhill?

 If you walk uphill, turn to page 86.

 If you walk downhill, turn to page 113.

You walk uphill, and soon you hear voices calling your name. Paige and the others are on the trail, searching for you. They're relieved to find you, but you can tell that Paige is upset. When you didn't catch up with her on Blue Sky Trail, she and the other girls had to start looking for you.

"The Nature Center staff is going to wonder where we are," Paige says. "They're expecting us to get to the campsite by dinnertime."

You have to hike quickly to reach the campsite before dark. When you finally make it, everyone's tired and sore. The Nature Center staff was just about to send out a search party.

You apologize to the staff, your cheeks burning. When Paige sees the expression on your face, she pulls you aside. "Hidden Hills Trail is really steep," she says. "I couldn't have hiked it quickly either."

"It was a big mistake," you confess. "I should have listened to the other girls when they said we should stick with the original path. I was trying too hard to impress them, but a smart leader respects other people's opinions. If I ever get another chance, I'll make better choices."

Paige smiles sympathetically. "I know you will," she says. Her confidence in you—and her forgiveness—makes you feel a little better. You hope that you'll get a second chance someday soon.

The End

You and Riley are on your way back to the fork. What seemed like a clear path on your way out isn't so clear on your way back. You come to another fork and then another, and soon you're totally lost!

You want to keep going, but Riley suggests that you both stay put and wait for Paige and the others to find you. "We shouldn't keep wandering around the woods," Riley says. "If we stay in one spot, Paige will find us."

You're not so sure that *anyone* will find you. Who knows how many wrong turns you've taken? Besides, after Paige chose you as her co-leader, it would be embarrassing to get lost in the forest. But you didn't listen to Riley's last idea (marking the trail), and that's how you ended up here.

If you work with Riley to come up with a new plan, turn to page 94.

If you give up on leading and decide that Riley knows best, turn to page 96.

You make your way through the brush and trees along the edge of the stream. Finally, you come to a log bridge that stretches across the stream to the other bank. Is that the bridge on your map?

The other girls think that trying to cross the logs is a mistake, but you're starting to get scared. You're lost, and no one knows where to look for you. You know for sure that the original trail was on the other side of the stream. You have to get across it to find Paige and the others.

"I'll go first," you say.

Map in hand, you step onto the logs. They're wet and slippery. You're about halfway across when you lose your footing and tumble into the cold water.

Turn to page 100.

Using teamwork, you, Shelby, and Riley are able to help Paige out of the ravine. Paige is definitely hurt. She wrenched her shoulder and sprained her wrist. She can't continue on the hike.

"I should have paid more attention to your rules," Paige says with a grimace. "Didn't you tell us to watch where we stepped?"

"I'm sure glad you figured out that we needed help," says Shelby.

The three of you help Paige back down the trail. When you reach the rest of the hikers, you leave Paige with them while you and Riley run to campus for help. A short while later, Nature Center staff members drive you into the woods on an ATV that will carry Paige back to campus.

No one wants to have the overnight without Paige. You promise the hikers that you'll plan another campout as soon as Paige is healed. Then you slip your backpack over your shoulders and guide the girls back to campus. This isn't how you expected the hike to go, but one thing is certain: you *have* become a leader.

The End

You're hot and tired as you make your way upstream. Neely's feet are so sore that she's limping. Logan is slowing down, too.

Finally you spot a bridge up ahead. Everyone cheers! With a new burst of energy, you cross the plank bridge and check your map.

"We're back on the original trail!" you say.

Neely looks the most relieved of all. She stops and leans against a tree. "Can we take a quick break?" she asks.

"Absolutely," you say. You all sit on the ground for a minute and eat a snack. A few minutes later, you hear voices!

Turn to page 95.

You look for something—anything—that will help you find your way. You stare at the sky. The sun is peeking out from behind a stray cloud or two. And then it hits you! You know that the sun is straight above you at noon, and then it starts to sink into the west. Maybe you can use the sun to help guide you back to the main trail.

"I'm sorry I didn't listen to you about marking the trail," you tell Riley.

She smiles kindly. "It did look pretty clear when we started out," she says.

You shake your head. "I still should have listened," you insist, "but I think we can find our way back to the fork if we work together. Are you with me?"

"Sure," says Riley. "Tell me your ideas."

 Turn to page 98.

Paige and the others are walking toward you. They're amazed that you beat them to this point in the trail.

Everyone's excited to hear about your adventures, and Shelby can't wait to show the girls a photo of the bear print on her digital camera. "And here's a deer," she says. "It was running so fast that all you see is a blur."

When you're safely at the campsite, you breathe a sigh of relief. It suddenly hits you that you could have gotten your friends into real trouble.

Paige pulls you aside for a private conversation. "It's a good thing you were able to find your way," she says. "No one would have known where to look for you."

You know Paige is right. You have a lot of apologies to make.

After Logan, Shelby, and Neely have had time to eat, you find them to let them know how sorry you are. "I was a terrible leader," you admit. "I should have listened better. I should have stayed on the original trail."

"No worries," Shelby tells you. "You promised us an adventure in the woods, and you delivered."

Neely agrees. "Only next time," she says, "NO BEARS!"

The End

The wait seems to last forever, but finally you hear voices calling your name and Riley's. Riley jumps to her feet and starts to yell. Soon Paige and Shelby are standing in front of you.

"What a confusing trail!" Paige says. "I'm so glad we found you."

"Me, too!" Riley says.

You respond with a quiet thank-you. You're completely mortified about getting lost.

As Paige and Shelby lead you back to the main trail, you notice that Paige does all the right things, like marking the trail and asking Shelby her opinion along the way. When you get back to the main trail, Paige takes the lead and you bring up the rear, convinced that no one will ever want to follow you again.

It's a long hike to the campsite, which gives you a lot of time to think about everything you did wrong. When you finally reach the campsite, you don't feel like joining in the fun. Instead, you slip into your tent.

You let yourself feel sad for a little while, thinking about all the things that you could have done better. You should have marked the trail, and you should have listened to Riley. Those are both things a smart leader would do.

You're so focused on your mistakes that you barely hear Paige step into the tent behind you. She sits down on your sleeping bag and gives you a kind smile.

"Do you want to talk about it?" she asks.

You shrug. You don't know what to say.

"I just made so many mistakes," you admit miserably.

"Maybe a few," says Paige. "But you did lots of things right, too. Those are the things you should focus on."

You hadn't thought about it that way, but Paige has a good point. It was your idea to split up into teams to explore both trails at the fork. And you were the one who remembered to bring trash bags, so you were able to clean up all that garbage in the clearing.

The truth is, you've learned a lot today—like how to focus on the positives. And one day, thanks to Paige, you're going to be a great leader!

The End

You share your ideas with Riley as you pull out your trail map. You think you can find the place on the map where the path forked. The trail you were hiking with Paige runs north. The path that you and Riley took to the left would have led you toward the west. So the main trail should be to the east.

"If we walk away from the sun," you say excitedly, "we should be heading east."

Riley gazes at the sky with a thoughtful expression. "Right," she says. "Or we could follow the clouds. I learned in science class that clouds almost always drift toward the east."

Together, using the sun and the clouds to guide you, you walk east—back in the direction of the trail. You find it just in time. Paige was about to send out a search party.

Your smart thinking under pressure impresses Paige. You surprised yourself, too. When you started the hike, you weren't sure you could be a good leader. Now you know you can be—when you listen to other people's ideas and work together.

The End

Splash!

You've fallen into the stream. It's not deep, but the current is strong. The map slips out of your hand. As you watch it float away and then sink underwater, your stomach sinks, too.

Now, not only are you totally lost, but you're also wet and cold. There are only a couple of hours of daylight left. Are you all going to have to spend the night out here?

You get to your feet and turn back to your friends. Reluctantly, you meet their eyes. You're afraid they might be angry with you for losing the map.

"Are you all right?" Logan yells.

You're relieved to see that your friends aren't angry. They're worried about you.

"I'm fine," you assure them.

Logan helps you out of the stream. Neely pulls an Innerstar U sweatshirt out of her backpack and helps you put it on. Shelby has a dry pair of shorts for you, too.

When your teeth stop chattering, you realize that your friends are waiting for you to tell them what to do next.

If you tell them you've run out of ideas and think you should all stay put, turn to page 102.

If you promise to keep trying to find your way, turn to page 104.

You all gather around Neely. She's found an old trail sign hidden in some brush. It reads "WATERFALL." The wooden arrow points to a narrow path.

"I didn't know there was a waterfall in the woods," Neely says.

"Neither did I," you answer.

You check the trail map. This path isn't marked. There's no waterfall on the map, either.

"A mysterious path," Logan says. "Let's explore!"

"Wait," you say cautiously. "We don't know how long that trail is or even if there *is* still a trail. It could take hours, or we could get lost. No one will know where to find us."

"Let's go just a little ways," Neely suggests. "If we don't see anything, we'll turn back."

You consider the options.

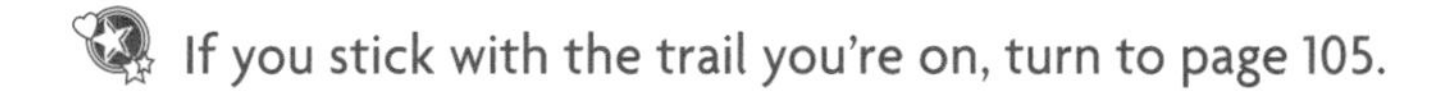
If you stick with the trail you're on, turn to page 105.

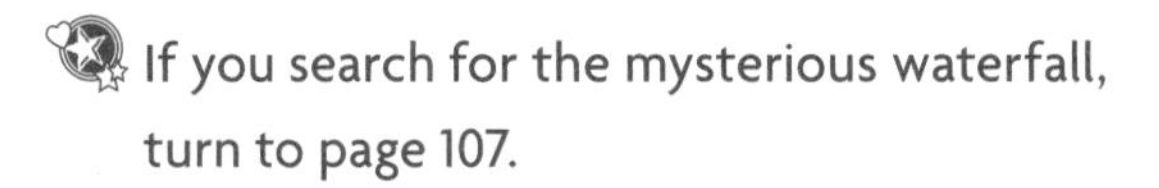
If you search for the mysterious waterfall, turn to page 107.

At this point, you realize that staying where you are is the smartest thing you can do. You're wet, cold, tired, and lost. Soon the girls will be hungry, too.

"I'm sorry I've been such a bad leader," you say.

Shelby smiles and squeezes your shoulders. "You only did what you thought was best," she says.

"I should have listened when you said we should stick with the original trail," you say to Neely. "I guess I was more worried about impressing everyone than I was about being safe."

"You did promise us an exciting adventure," Neely says. "I'm sure the other girls didn't get to see a bear's paw print."

You appreciate that your friends are trying to make you feel better, but you know you failed as a leader. "I think the only thing to do now is to wait here to be found," you say sadly.

Neely leans against you and starts to hum the school song. Shelby and Logan start singing along. After a while, you can't help but start singing, too.

Singing lifts everyone's spirits, and soon you're singing loudly enough to be heard by a search party. The next thing you know, you hear someone calling you from the other side of the stream. It's Paige and a small group of girls and staff.

"Paige!" you yell.

"We're rescued!" Neely says.

"Woo-hoo!" Logan shouts.

Paige cups her hands around her mouth so that you can hear her from across the stream. She tells you that if you hike upstream a short ways, you'll find the real bridge.

You and your friends hike around a bend in the stream, and there it is! A wooden bridge stretches over the cold water. Paige is waiting on the other side.

"We expected you at the campsite a couple of hours ago," Paige says. "When you didn't show up, we thought we'd better look for you."

"It's my fault," you tell her. "I wanted to impress you by taking the harder trail, and instead I got us lost. I didn't make good choices. And I didn't listen to the other girls' ideas. I wasn't a very smart leader."

Paige is surprisingly understanding. "Next time, you'll do better," she says with a smile.

"Next time?" you ask. Then you realize she's right. You've learned a lot from your mistakes. If you ever lead another hike, you *know* you'll do better. You hope you get the chance.

The End

You might be wet and cold, but you can't just sit around and wait for help to find you. It's your fault your friends are lost in the woods, and it's your responsibility to make sure they're safe—especially now that you know there are bears in the area!

For the second time today, you climb a tree to try to figure out where you are. The sun is low in the sky on your left. You know the sun sets in the west, which means north must be straight ahead.

The original trail leading to the campsite ran north. If you could just find the bridge and get to the other side of the stream, you could walk north to the campsite.

You close your eyes and try to picture the sunken trail map. The bridge was near a big bend in the stream. You open your eyes again. Could it be that bend you see in the distance? You'll have to investigate to be sure.

Turn to page 108.

You tell your friends that you think it's best to stick with the trail you're on.

"Can you take a picture of the waterfall sign?" you ask Shelby. "Paige will want to know about it for sure. Maybe we can hike this trail on our way back to campus tomorrow."

You mark the spot on your map before leading the girls back onto Hidden Hills Trail. It's downhill now and much easier to navigate. Before long, you've reached the point where this trail meets up with Blue Sky Trail.

When you get there, you're not sure what to do. Have you beat Paige and the others to this spot? Or have they already gone on to the campsite? You wait a few minutes, and then you hear voices. Paige and Riley led the other girls to the campsite, and now they're walking back to try to find you.

You can't wait to tell Paige about the mysterious waterfall sign.

Turn to page 106.

"Wow," Paige says, checking out Shelby's photo. "I've hiked that trail a few times, and I've never come across that sign."

"Do you think there really is a waterfall?" you ask.

"There's only one way to find out," Paige says. "We'll have to plan another hike for next weekend! You can lead the way."

That night over dinner and songs around the campfire, your thoughts keep drifting back to the waterfall. You're so excited about the next hike that you can hardly sleep.

In the morning, after you've had breakfast and cleaned up the campsite, you're the first one to step onto the trail to lead your friends home. When you left Innerstar U yesterday, you were a little unsure about your skills as a leader. Now you know not only that you can lead but that you love to do it. And with a whole forest to explore, there'll be lots of opportunities!

The End

You decide to search for the mysterious waterfall. Just think how excited Paige will be when you tell her what you've found!

You take the lead. You walk along quietly, listening to the sounds of the woods and the gentle shuffling of feet behind you. The trees are so tall and dense that they block out the sun. You wonder if this is what it was like for Native Americans so many years ago.

You pass a maple tree, its trunk covered with moss. "Wow," you whisper to your friends. "These usually grow in wet areas. We must be getting closer."

This path grows narrower. You're breaking through brambles and vines and even a spiderweb or two. And then you feel something else—a giant spider on your arm!

If you scream, turn to page 109.

If you shake off the spider and keep going, turn to page 116.

You climb down out of the tree and stand in front of your tired, hungry, scared friends. "I know you probably don't trust me after I've been such a bad leader," you say, "but I'll do everything I can to find our way. I'm going to scout upstream for a short distance and see what I can find."

"I don't think you should go alone," Neely says. She winces as she gets to her feet.

"I'll be fine," you tell her. "I'm going only as far as the next bend. I think the bridge is just past it, but I want to be sure before I make you hike anymore. You need a rest."

Shelby makes you promise to stay within shouting distance, and then you make your way along the stream bank. You round the bend, and there's the bridge!

If you run back for your friends, turn to page 110.

If you cross the bridge, turn to page 112.

Your friends don't know why you screamed, but they start screaming, too. Pretty soon, all three of them are running back to the main trail. You have no choice but to follow.

"It was just a spider!" you call after your friends.

You're all breathless when you reach the trail.

"It was just a spider," you say again. "But maybe we'd better stick with this trail and come back to explore the waterfall another day."

"That path was a little spooky," Neely says with a shaky laugh. "I started imagining we were the last people on earth." She rubs the goose bumps on her arms.

Turn to page 114.

Your friends are just as excited about the bridge as you are. That bridge will lead you to the original trail!

It's almost dark when you reach the campsite—and a very worried Paige. She's a little angry that you took a different trail, because no one knew where to look for you. But she's impressed that you found your way here.

You know you made a lot of mistakes, but you also learned some good lessons—like how important it is to tell someone where you'll be in the woods *and* to listen to other girls' ideas. Those are things a smart leader would do.

Later, as you all sit around the campfire, Neely reads her ghost story. She tries to sound spooky, but she giggles so much that everyone else cracks up, too. When she's done, Logan points out the constellations in the night sky.

Over the crackling fire, Shelby says to you, "If we split into two groups again tomorrow, I want to go with you."

"Are you kidding? After I got you lost?" you say.

Shelby laughs. "You did, but you also got us found again," she says. "You were a great leader."

The End

You run across the bridge. You want to be absolutely sure you're on the right track before you get your friends too excited.

You're looking down the trail when you hear a rumbling sound. A few seconds later, an ATV from Innerstar U comes into view. Paige and the Nature Center staff must have sent out a search party. You've been rescued!

As soon as you let the search party know you're safe, you run back to find Shelby, Logan, and Neely. They're leaning against a tree, eating the last of the trail mix.

"I found the bridge!" you shout. "And the Nature Center staff—they're looking for us."

After a round of cheers, the girls slip on their backpacks and head upstream to the bridge and the waiting ATV.

Turn to page 115.

Your friends are tired, so you all agree to hike downhill. You try to hurry the girls along, even though everyone's legs and feet are sore. You're still hoping to reach camp before dark. "Paige is going to be worried," you say.

"Wait, I think I hear something," Logan says.

You can hear it, too—voices! "Yay!" you cheer. "The campsite must be close by."

Finally, you round a bend. When Logan, Neely, and Shelby see what's in front of you, they burst out laughing. You've led them right back to the Nature Center!

You try to laugh, too, but really you want to cry. There's no way you'll have the energy to hike out to the campsite now. You're going to miss the campout entirely.

The first thing you do is find the Nature Center staff so that they can let Paige know you're safe. Then you head over to the Star Student Center for dinner. You feel terrible about letting your friends down.

Shelby can see that you're upset. "We had a great day," she tells you. "We all wanted to go on the hike to spend time with you—it's okay that we never made it to the campsite."

"Really?" you ask.

"Really," Neely says, pulling you into a hug.

You shake your head and laugh. "The next time I lead anyone anywhere," you say, "I'm sticking to the plan!"

The End

Everyone laughs about your run-in with the "spooky spider." Neely starts making up a story about a wicked witch who uses a giant spider to keep the enchanted waterfall a secret. You know it's not true, but the hair on your arms stands up.

"Secretly, the waterfall longs to be discovered," Neely continues. "It's our duty to break the witch's spell and free the waterfall."

You giggle. Neely's story is so entertaining that you barely realize it when the trail starts heading downhill. The route gets faster and easier. Before long, you reach the point where this trail joins up with the original. You're just a short way from the campsite!

Everyone cheers when you arrive. The first thing you do when you get there is tell Paige about the mysterious waterfall.

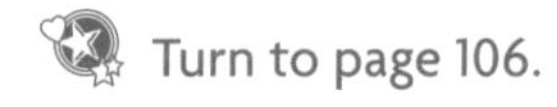
Turn to page 106.

When you ride into camp on the ATV, everyone is relieved to see you. The first thing you do is thank Paige for sending out the search party.

You can tell that Paige is disappointed in you. "No one knew where to look when you weren't on the trail," she says. "You could have spent the whole night wandering around in the woods."

Paige is right—things could have ended very differently. After talking with her, you're way too embarrassed to hang out with the other girls. You slip into your tent and hide until dinner, thinking of all the bad decisions you made.

During dinner around the campfire, you pull Paige aside. "I learned a lot about leadership today," you tell her. "Mostly I learned what not to do. I never should have switched trails without telling someone, and I should have listened to the other girls' opinions."

"I made a lot of mistakes my first time, too," Paige tells you. "You did a great job of finding your way back, though. I'd want you with me if *I* ever got lost."

You manage a smile. "Well," you say, "you might get your chance tomorrow." Paige giggles, and now you know that everything is going to be okay. Tomorrow is a new day—a chance to be a better leader and friend.

The End

You shake off the spider, reminding yourself that spiders play an important role in nature. You try to focus on the trail ahead.

The path gets steep again. Your friends are breathing hard as you all struggle through the brush that has grown over this ancient path. You hear a woodpecker drumming against the bark of a tree. It stops and calls to you. Its song sounds like laughter.

Finally, the path starts to go downhill again. You can see another trail marker for the waterfall. "Yay! We're on the right track," you say.

Pretty soon you can hear a soft *whooshing* sound. It grows louder and louder.

You step into a clearing, and there it is—a gorgeous waterfall. The water rushes down a rock wall, landing in a bubbling pool at the bottom.

Shelby gasps and starts taking pictures. Neely sits down to sketch the scene. You and Logan just stand still, taking it all in.

You wish you could stay here all night, but the sun is sinking in the sky. Paige and the others will be worried if you don't get to the campsite soon. You borrow Shelby's camera and take one last picture of your friends and the waterfall before turning back to the trail.

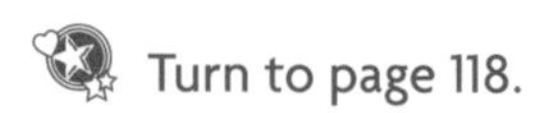
Turn to page 118.

Paige and the others are waiting for you when you reach the campsite. "I was just about to send out a search party," she says.

"You won't believe where we've been!" you tell her. You share your afternoon adventures. Everyone oohs and aahs over Shelby's photos and Neely's sketches.

Paige is a little upset that you took a different trail. "We were worried about you," she says. "If you'd gotten lost or hurt, we wouldn't have even known where to look."

Oops, you hadn't thought about that. Your shoulders slump. "I'm sorry," you tell Paige. "I wanted to prove to you that I could be a good leader after my bad decision to bring Honey along. I guess I made an even bigger mess of things."

Paige smiles. "It's okay, now that everyone's safe," she says. "And I can't believe you found a waterfall. I've hiked Hidden Hills Trail before, and I've never seen that sign."

After looking at Shelby's photos, everyone else wants to see the waterfall, too. You change your route for the hike home tomorrow so that they can.

After a delicious dinner, s'mores, and songs around the campfire, you're ready to sleep. You and Paige crawl into the tent that you're sharing.

"I'm excited about seeing the waterfall," Paige whispers. "I'm counting on you to lead the way."

The next morning, you and Paige help clean up the campground. Then you slip your backpack over your shoulders and step confidently onto the trail.

You feel as if you're in an enchanted forest as you lead the girls uphill along Hidden Hills Trail. When you come to the waterfall sign, you proudly show it to Paige.

"That's really hard to spot," she says.

"We needed an artist like Neely to find it," you say. "She was looking for hidden wildflowers, not a hidden waterfall!"

You lead the girls up the steep, overgrown path and back down the hill toward the waterfall. This time, you know exactly where you're going.

"I can hear it!" Paige says. Her brown eyes flash with excitement as you lead her and the others around a bend.

Paige gasps when she sees the water rushing down the rock wall, swirling and bubbling at the bottom. "It's gorgeous," she says.

You feel as if you've given Paige a wonderful gift. And you have. But she's given you one, too. She has shown you how to become a true leader.

The End